D1506327

The
Chicken
and The
Worm

by Page McBrier

Illustrated by
Rick Peterson

HEIFER
INTERNATIONAL

www.heifer.org

Heifer International
1 World Avenue, Little Rock, AR, 72202, United States
www.heifer.org

Heifer International is no stranger to caring for the
Earth. Since 1944, Heifer has helped more than 9.2 million
families in more than 125 countries move toward greater
self-reliance through gifts of livestock and training in
environmentally sound agriculture. The impact of each
initial gift is multiplied as recipients agree to "pass on the
gift" by giving one or more of their animal's offspring or the
equivalent to another in need. Visit Heifer.org to learn more
about ways your family can help end hunger and poverty.

The Chicken and The Worm

Text copyright © 2008 by Page McBrier

Illustrations copyright © 2008 by Rick Peterson

Designed and produced by
  Verve Marketing & Design, Chadds Ford, PA 19317 USA

Printed on 10% post-consumer paper,
using lead-free, soy ink: 20% soy or vegetable content.

Text is set in Triplex, Display type is Zephyr

Printed in the U.S.A.

ISBN 978-0-9798439-2-1

Description of the work: The Chicken and The Worm is a children's
book for Pre-K ages 4-6 years old. It is a tale of warmth, friendship,
innovation and humor. Page McBrier, award-winning author of
Beatrice's Goat, and illustrator Rick Peterson have created a story
that could change the world...or certainly your garden. Warm,
colorful illustrations and straight-forward, often humorous dialog
introduce young readers to the idea that even the smallest creatures
can work together to care for the Earth.

All rights reserved. No part of this book may be reproduced or
transmitted in any form or by any means, electronic or mechanical,
including photocopying, recording, or by any information storage
and retrieval systems, without written permission from the publisher.

For the students at Dunbar Gardens,
who introduced me to the chickens and worms.
~P.M.

For August and Elsa, and the critters they love.
~R.P.

I am a **chicken.**

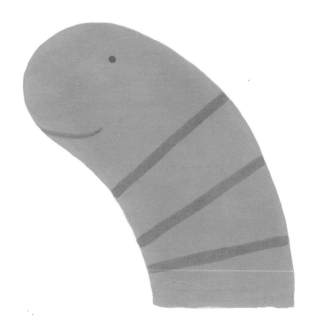

I am a worm.

We come in many shapes, sizes, and colors.

So do we.

I happen to be
a Rhode Island Red.

RHODE ISLAND RED

And *I* am
a red wiggler.

I live in a coop.

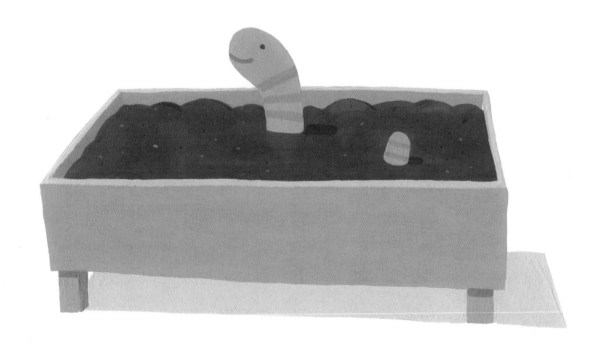

My home is a wooden bin.

My nest is made of cozy straw.

I cuddle into strips of moist newspaper.

My eggs are a beautiful brown.

My cocoons look like
tiny lemon drops.

I lay an egg
almost every day.

hello Tuesday!

I create
two or three
cocoons a week.
Each cocoon holds
three to four babies.

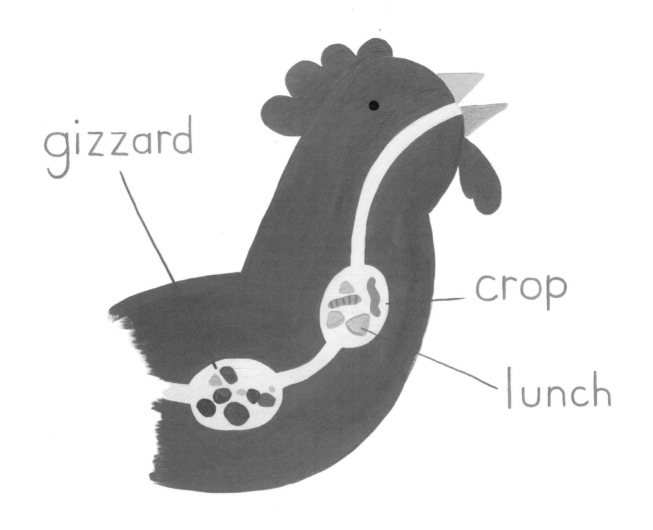

gizzard

crop

lunch

Chickens have no teeth. Our food is stored in our crops and chopped up in our gizzards.

hat

crop

gizzard

Worms have crops and gizzards, too.

We eat
beans, watermelon,
grapes, corn,
pizza crusts,
pecans . . .

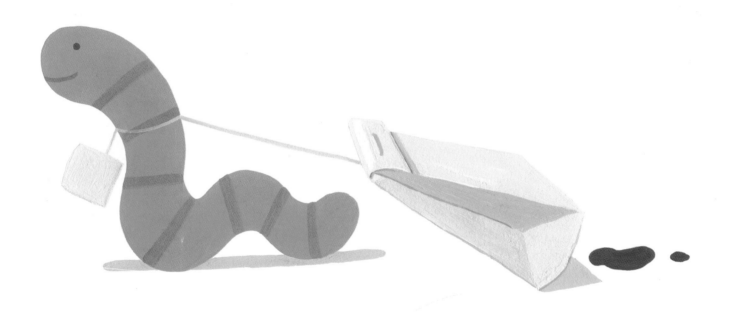

. . . yes, yes, yes, yes, yes, yes, . . .
AND tea bags and coffee grounds.

DO NOT
feed a chicken honey buns!

DO NOT
feed a worm hamburgers!

Did you know that my manure
helps plants and vegetables grow?

Mine too. Worm manure is called castings.
Red wigglers make the world's best worm castings.

Sometimes I get put into
the chicken tiller to search
for bugs. My sharp beak
and claws help loosen
the soil so plants can grow.

28

My cousin, the earthworm, does the same thing
as it tunnels deep underground.

A worm with a beak and claws?! Yikes.

**No, silly. I was trying to say that
both chickens and worms help care for the Earth.**

You've got that right!

Who knew worms could be so special?

34

Who knew chickens could be so important?

The End.